Lily's New Home

by Paula Yoo

illustrated by Shirley Ng-Benitez

Lee & Low Books Inc.   New York

For the always curious Griffin, with much love from Auntie Paula—P.Y.

With love to mom, who made our house a true home—S.N-B.

Copyright © 2016 Lee & Low Books Inc.
All rights reserved. No part of this book may be reproduced, transmitted, or stored in
an information retrieval system in any form or by any means, electronic, mechanical,
photocopying, recording, or otherwise, without written permission from the publisher.
LEE & LOW BOOKS Inc., 95 Madison Avenue, New York, NY 10016
leeandlow.com
Book design by Maria Mercado
Book production by The Kids at Our House
The illustrations are rendered digitally
Manufactured in China by Imago, January 2016
Printed on paper from responsible sources
(hc) 10 9 8 7 6 5 4 3 2 1
(pb) 10 9 8 7 6 5 4 3 2 1
First Edition

Library of Congress Cataloging-in-Publication Data
Yoo, Paula.
Lily's new home / by Paula Yoo; illustrated by Shirley Ng-Benitez.
     pages cm. — (Dive into reading ; 1)
Summary: "Lily and her parents move to a new home in New York City. Everything is so new and
different, which makes Lily even more homesick"— Provided by publisher.
ISBN 978-1-62014-249-3 (hardcover : alk. paper) ISBN 978-1-62014-258-5 (pbk. : alk. paper)
[1. Moving, Household—Fiction. 2. Homesickness—Fiction. 3. African Americans—Fiction. 4. New
York (N.Y.)—Fiction.] I. Ng-Benitez, Shirley, illustrator. II. Title.
PZ7.Y8156Li 2016   [E]—dc23   2015029137

Contents

A New Home

"We're here!" said Lily's dad.
Lily looked at their new home.
"There is no front yard," said Lily.
"There are no flowers."

"The city is different," said Lily's mom.
"But you will like it here."
Lily was not so sure.

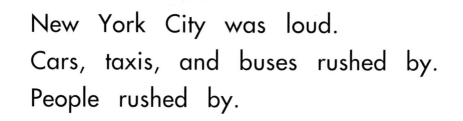

New York City was loud.
Cars, taxis, and buses rushed by.
People rushed by.

Lily missed her old home.

Two boys sat on the steps.
One boy read a book.
Another boy played a drum.
BAM!

The boy closed his book
and went inside.
Lily hoped to see him again.
She loved to read too.

Exploring

Lily and her parents walked down their new street.
A woman sold flowers and fruit from a small store.
Lily smelled some flowers.
Her mom bought some fruit.

Two girls jumped rope.
"That looks fun," said Lily.
The two girls waved to Lily.
Lily hoped to see them again.

Lily and her parents walked
by a garden.
"This is a public garden,"
said Lily's mom.
"What does *public* mean?"
asked Lily.

"*Public* means the garden
is for everyone," said her mom.
"Everyone?" asked Lily.
"Yes," said Lily's mom.
"The garden is for all of us."

Lily and her parents ate
pizza for lunch.
"This is a big slice," said Lily.

Lily took a bite of her pizza.
"Yum!" she said.

After lunch they looked
in store windows.
"What does this sign say?"
asked Lily.
"It says *welcome* in Spanish,"
said her dad.

They saw a store with dresses.
"These dresses are from India,"
said Lily's mom.

Lily and her parents walked
into a store.
They saw masks and clothes.
Lily's dad put on a mask.

"This mask is from Kenya," he said.
"Kenya is a country in Africa."
"Wow!" said Lily.

The Library

Lily still missed her old home.
Then she saw a sign
that she knew: LIBRARY.

Lily was excited.
"It looks like our old library,"
she said.

Lily got her own library card.
She got her own library books
to take home.

"Do you need help?" asked Lily's dad.
"No, thank you," said Lily.
"I can carry these books
all the way home."

Lily skipped home.
She did not drop her books.

Then Lily saw the boy reading
on the steps.
"I like to read too," said Lily.
"I'm new here. My name is Lily."

The boy looked up and smiled.
"I'm Pablo," he said.
"Do you want to read with me?"

"Yes," said Lily.
"We can share our books."

Lily and Pablo sat on the steps.
They read their books.
They shared their books.

Lily had a friend.
She was starting to like
her new home.

Have more fun with this book!

Lily misses her old home. Make a list of all the ways her new home is different from her old home. Then write a story about your home.

Lily loves to read. What are your favorite things to do? Draw pictures of yourself doing some of your favorite things.

At the end of the story, Lily makes a new friend. Think about a time when you made a new friend. How did you feel? Write a letter to your new friend about what you like to do with him or her, and why.